The Sailor's Tale

PRAISE FOR *STORYSHARES*

"One of the brightest innovators and game-changers in the education industry."
– Forbes

"Your success in applying research-validated practices to promote literacy serves as a valuable model for other organizations seeking to create evidence-based literacy programs."

- Library of Congress

"We need powerful social and educational innovation, and Storyshares is breaking new ground. The organization addresses critical problems facing our students and teachers. I am excited about the strategies it brings to the collective work of making sure every student has an equal chance in life."
– Teach For America

"Around the world, this is one of the up-and-coming trailblazers changing the landscape of literacy and education."
- International Literacy Association

"It's the perfect idea. There's really nothing like this. I mean wow, this will be a wonderful experience for young people."   - Andrea Davis Pinkney, Executive Director, Scholastic

"Reading for meaning opens opportunities for a lifetime of learning. Providing emerging readers with engaging texts that are designed to offer both challenges and support for each individual will improve their lives for years to come. Storyshares is a wonderful start."
- David Rose, Co-founder of CAST & UDL

The Sailor's Tale

Jennie Ford

STORYSHARES

Story Share, Inc.
New York. Boston. Philadelphia

Storyshares
Story Share, Inc.
24 N. Bryn Mawr Avenue #340
Bryn Mawr, PA 19010-3304
www.storyshares.org

Inspiring reading with a new kind of book.

Interest Level: Middle School
Grade Level Equivalent: 2.8

9781642611199

Book design by Storyshares

Printed in the United States of America

Storyshares Presents

1

The sky was getting dark and the wind was picking up. I should have been home an hour ago.

I had been at my friend Charlotte's house and let the time get away from me. It was a good four miles to my house by road, but only a few minutes' walk if I cut through the woods.

I walked fast. The wind was whipping the tops of the trees, making them look like giant paint brushes coloring the sky. A loud clap of thunder made me jump. A drop of rain as big as a quarter hit my face.

"Here it comes," I said out loud. I picked up my pace until I came to a clearing in the woods. This is the part of the trail that we feared, dreaded. Here in this clearing sat the Sailor's house.

I stopped. The rain was coming down in buckets. I looked and didn't see the old Sailor, or his wild dog. There was another bright flash of lightning, and I swear I felt the heat of it. Immediately, a loud boom of thunder shook the ground.

The Sailor's wild dog started barking. I closed my eyes and ran as I fast as could past that horrible house.

When I knew I was well past it, I stopped and checked behind me. The mean dog's barking grew louder.

I ran until I came to the clearing across from my house. I caught my breath and hurried the rest of the way home, looking back often, making sure the old Sailor wasn't following me home.

I threw the door open and ran straight to the bathroom to dry off.

My brother, Tony, looked up from the TV. "You're getting the floor wet. Mama's going to kill you."

"Shut up," I told him.

He shrugged his shoulders and went back to his show. I managed to get out of my wet clothes and put on my pajamas. The sky was so dark, it made the four o'clock afternoon feel like late evening.

The wind blew fiercely and the rain pelted loudly on our tin roof. I grabbed a towel and started wiping up the puddles of water I had made during my wild dash to the bathroom.

BAM!

A loud noise came from the front of the house.

"What was that?" Tony asked, sitting straight up in the recliner.

BAM! We heard again.

I was frozen in place, clutching the soggy towel close to me. Tony and I looked at each other, our eyes wide.

"Turn the TV down," I whispered to him. We were locked in place, straining our ears to hear anything.

"Is someone at the front door?" Tony asked softly.

A loud clap of thunder shook the house, making us both shriek. We ran to my room, locked the door, and sat on my bed, each of us hugging a pillow close.

"Tony, I think the old Sailor followed me home." My voice shook as I whispered.

Tony's eyes grew even bigger.

We heard no more loud sounds except the rain, wind, and thunder. Still, we stayed huddled in my room until we heard Mama's voice.

"Kids, where are you?"

We bolted from my room to hug her.

"Someone was trying to get in the front door," I said.

"What? What are you talking about?"

"We kept hearing banging in the front of the house. It was really loud," I told her.

"Oh? Let's go take a look," Mama said.

Tony and I both clutched onto her as we walked to the dark foyer that led to the front door. No one ever used this door, except an occasional salesman or preacher. Mama switched on the foyer light and opened the big, heavy door. She looked around the front porch before opening the screen door next.

When she walked out onto the porch, the heavy rain blew in.

"I don't see anything... There's nothing out here, kids."

"What's that?" I asked.

The three of us looked out across the field from our front yard and saw a big, black dog running toward the woods.

"That's the Sailor's dog." I said, and a shudder ran through my body.

2

Mama tapped lightly on my door. "Amelia, can I come in?"

"Yes," I said. "What's up?"

Her hair was pulled back in a long ponytail. She had put on a touch of makeup and a small bit of perfume. She looked so pretty. She was leaving for her job at the doctor's office, where she was a nursing assistant.

"Are you ready for school?" she asked.

"Almost," I said. "We've got twenty minutes until the bus gets here," I reminded her.

She sat down on my bed and patted the spot next to her for me to sit as well.

"Amelia, you know I am so proud of you. I don't know what I'd do without you. You help me a lot. Thank you," she said.

"You're welcome, Mama. I don't really do that much."

"You do. You help me take care of your little brother. I wish I didn't have to be gone so much, but we need the money. I hope you understand." Her eyes looked sad.

"It's okay, Mama, I understand."

"I'm going to take a job at the seafood restaurant in Morehead City on the weekends. I will be working different hours, sometimes at night. I don't want to, but I need to. It won't be this way forever, just for the summer season."

She looked at me, wanting me to be okay, to not be upset.

"Mama, me and Tony will be fine. I just don't like you working so much. I hate it."

"I'll be okay as long as you and Tony are okay. You know, we've got to have a new furnace before winter. Remember how we just about froze last year?" Mama asked with a smile.

"Well, I kind of liked all of us huddling together at night in your bed," I said.

Mama got up and touched my face with her hand. "I've got to go. I'll see you guys around five." She turned to leave but then remembered one last thing. "Amelia, I do believe you and Tony heard something the other night. I know you guys were scared. It was storming something awful and the wind was up. I'm thinking something just blew and hit the house. The old Sailor is an oddball, but I'm sure he isn't mean or dangerous. He was old and feeble, last I saw him. I did ask Mr. Claude and Miss Mary Ann if I could give you their number to call if you need them, though, or if you get scared. They said that you could call and Mr. Claude would be right here. I set their number by the phone."

Mr. Claude, I thought to myself. He and his wife were our closest neighbors, about a mile up the road.

Mama wants me to feel at ease because Mr. Claude will protect us?

Mr. Claude was the oldest man alive that I had ever seen in my life. His thin, little body was stooped and twisted. He walked crookedly, even with a cane. His head bobbed up and down and his hands shook.

"Thank you, Mama, that's good to know."

She smiled and went to work.

"Come on, Tony, we gotta catch the bus," I yelled through the house.

Tony came running. He really was an okay kid. At nine years old, he didn't complain or whine too much, just kind of went with the flow.

"So, Tony," I said as we made our way to the bus stop. "We don't have to worry about getting scared anymore. Mama has someone that we can call to come to our rescue."

"She does?" he said.

"Yes, she left Mr. Claude's number for us to call. He said he'd come right over."

"Mr. Claude?" Tony asked. "Is he still alive?"

3

As much as I hated my mother working two jobs, my life could've been worse.

Mrs. Womack was my friend Charlotte's mama. She was a stay-at-home housewife. I never saw her without an apron on or an oven mitt on her hand. The smell of homemade goodies always poured out of her kitchen, and her lovely house was spotless. But Mrs. Womack was wacky.

"Come in, Amelia," Mrs. Womack smiled through red lips. "Please leave your shoes on the porch, dear."

"Oh, yes ma'am, I almost forgot," I said, pulling off my tennis shoes.

"Are you hungry, dear?" she asked.

"No, ma'am. I'm fine."

"I just worry about you and Tony so much, what with your mother never home and all."

"Me and Tony are fine, thank you. Is Charlotte home?" I asked.

"Charlotte! Company!" Her voice sounded like fingernails running down a chalk board.

"Mom, I'm not deaf," Charlotte said as she came down the polished steps. "Hey, Amelia, let me grab my shoes. I'll be right back."

Mrs. Womack smiled at me while looking me up and down. "I hear you and Tony had a scare the other night during the big storm," she said, still smiling.

"It was just the wind, I suppose. We just got carried away," I said.

"Randy says you thought it was the old Sailor."

"Well, you know how Tony and Randy get scared. It was nothing." I wished that Charlotte would hurry up.

"Mother, my little brother and her little brother are both idiots," Charlotte said, finally ready to go.

"The old Sailor has always been a strange man, walking in town with those horrid tattoos," Mrs. Womack continued. "He's a Johnson, you know. That whole family is loony. Story is, he brought a young, Spanish wife home from one of his journeys. His family never took to her. It has been told that the whole lot of them shunned her. She was seen coming to town, shopping, walking the fields, picking flowers or gathering blackberries, until one day, she just disappeared. No one knows what happened to her, or where she went. The family died off, eventually, all but the old Sailor, and there he stays, at the Johnson place."

"Bye, Mom. See you later," Charlotte said, grabbing my arm and heading for the door.

"Charlotte, don't be long!" her mother yelled in her screechy voice.

"My God, let's get out of here," Charlotte said.

4

Charlotte and I went to our private hideout. It was an old barn behind her grandfather's house. It once housed horses and had a high hay loft.

This was our place to listen to the radio and read our Tiger Beat magazines. Here, we talked about our dreams, our hopes for the future. We plotted our schemes and bared our souls in the loft. What we said here stayed here. It was our refuge.

We entered the old barn and immediately heard a radio humming out some muffled tunes.

We looked at each other. *What?*

"Randy, are you in here?" Charlotte yelled, sounding too much like her mother.

The radio quickly turned off. We heard the scuffling of feet. Two heads peeked down by the ladder. Randy and Tony had found our private lair.

"Get down here right now!" Charlotte screamed.

The boys obeyed.

"We found this place fair and square, Charlotte," Randy said defiantly.

"This is our place," Tony added.

"Ah, no," Charlotte said. "That's where you are wrong. This is our place and it has always been our place. So you little twerps need to beat it."

"Well, I'm telling Mother," Randy said. "You can't have this whole barn. Me and Tony get half."

Charlotte was red with anger. She took a few breaths before she spoke. "I don't think you two babies remember last Halloween, do you?"

That was all it took. We had held last Halloween over their heads for about a year now.

I tried to look as serious as Charlotte, but almost laughed. Randy's smug determination faded from his face. Tony held his head down in shame.

"Beat it, babies," Charlotte huffed.

They knew they were defeated. I wondered just how long we could play that card.

Last Halloween, Randy and Tony were both given little cardboard boxes by their second-grade teacher. Those boxes were supposed to be used to collect coins while trick-or-treating, to donate to underprivileged children. They'd done quite well in collecting. But instead of turning their money in, they decided to walk to Cameron's store. We happened upon them sitting in Tony's room, reading comic books and eating candy.

"Tony, have you got the basketball?" I asked, walking into his room. They'd both jumped up with chocolate-covered faces. "Where did you get all this stuff?"

"Look," Charlotte had said, pointing. There sat their two empty cardboard boxes.

"You didn't turn in your charity money?" I asked.

They'd both just stared, wide-eyed.

"Are you kidding me? You spent charity money on yourselves?" Charlotte added.

Both boys had looked like they were going to cry. That's when Charlotte and I looked at each other and grinned.

"You better be ashamed, both of you. I can't even look at you. Mama wouldn't be able to show her face in public if she knew her son would steal from the poor," I'd said.

"You know," Charlotte had shook her head, side to side, slowly and dramatically, "Some little kid is hungry right now cause of you, maybe even starving to death. I can't even think about it." Charlotte had also put her hand to her face like she was going to cry.

"It's okay, Charlotte." I'd patted her back. "I hope you two enjoy your comic books and candy," I'd said, solemnly.

Then we'd left them, clutching their Hershey bars, their heads hung low.

5

Summer break turned out to be not that great for me. It was filled with babysitting Tony. I was responsible for him. I had to make sure he was okay. That was such a big responsibility for a thirteen-year-old girl, but Mama needed me. It was the least I could do.

I woke up one morning to the sound of clattering from the old shed behind our house. I rose and rubbed my eyes and went to investigate. Tony was busy pulling a rusty sickle out.

"What are you doing?" I asked, in my sleepy, raspy voice.

"I'm getting tools to build our fort," he said.

"What fort?"

"The fort Randy and I are building in the woods. You and Charlotte can have your old barn. We're going to have our own place."

"Okay," I said, and went back to bed.

I woke up to the telephone ringing and the sun shining through my bedroom window.

"Hello?" I said, half asleep.

"Did you just wake up?" It was Mama, sounding annoyed.

"No," I lied.

"Where's your brother?" she asked

"Ah, he's building a fort in the woods with Randy," I answered.

"Did he have breakfast?"

I looked in the kitchen sink and saw a dirty bowl.

"Yes, he had cereal," I answered.

"Okay. There's lunch meat and bread. Make sure he eats lunch. I will be there a little past five."

"I will. Have a good day, Mama."

I hung up and heard a knock on my door. It was Charlotte.

"Get your bathing suit on, we're going swimming," she said. "I've got the four-wheeler, and we're going to Radio Island." She smiled.

"I've got to watch Tony, and I just woke up."

"He's fine. He and Randy are building a fort. Go change, I'll wait," Charlotte said, plopping on the couch.

I went to my room and searched through my drawers. My bathing suit from last year was old and ratty and getting a little snug. I changed into it and put a big t-shirt over it. I needed a new one, but did not want to worry Mama over anything else. I brushed my hair and pulled it back into a ponytail.

"I'm ready," I said.

Our short swim at Radio Island turned into several hours. It's a small inlet with slow and lazy water. The beach was warm, the day pleasant. I lay drying in the lowering sun.

Tony! I remembered.

"We have to go, Charlotte. I need to check on Tony!" I said as I sat up.

"He should be home. Randy had Cub Scouts at three," Charlotte mumbled, half asleep from the warm sun.

"I've got to go and check on him, Charlotte."

I thought of how Tony had begged Mama to let him join the Scouts, too. She couldn't afford the cost of uniforms and dues, and couldn't get him to meetings. I remember how he'd lowered his head and said it was okay, even though his heart was broken.

"I need to go, Charlotte, please." The short ride home seemed to take forever. I jumped off the four-wheeler and ran into the house.

"Tony? Tony? Are you here?" I yelled out. He wasn't home and it was four-thirty. I walked outside and searched the fields around our house.

"Tony! Tony!" I yelled.

I went inside and called Charlotte's house. Mrs. Womack answered.

"Hello?"

"Mrs. Womack? Is Tony there?" I asked as calmly as I could.

"Why, no, Amelia, he's not. Randy went to Cub Scouts. I haven't seen him."

"Oh, thank you, Mrs. Womack."

"Are you okay, Amelia?" she asked.

"Yes, fine, thank you," I said. I hung up the phone.

I ran back outside and saw Tony limping across the field.

"Tony!"

I ran to him. He was crying and shaking. He had cuts and scrapes and his clothes were torn.

"Amelia, he tried to get me. He tried to grab me. I couldn't get away."

"Who, Tony, who?" I grabbed and hugged him. "What happened? Who grabbed you?" I was shaking now, too.

"The Sailor," he said. "The old Sailor."

6

I took Tony into the bathroom to wash up his scratches. He was inconsolable. His whole body shook as he sobbed.

"It's okay now, Tony," I kept telling him. "You are home and safe. You're okay now."

"He tried to get me, Amelia. He told me to get off of his land. I tried, I really did. I got hung up in the vines and couldn't get free. He tried to grab me." He sobbed on my shoulder.

"Shh, shh," I said, as I rubbed his head. "You're okay now, you're fine."

I cried tears of sadness and guilt for not being there to protect him.

"The dark lady, she came. The dark lady helped me. She opened the bushes and told me to run. She helped me."

The back porch door opened, then, and we heard the rustle of grocery bags.

"I'm home!" Mama announced.

Tony and I looked at each other. She was going to be upset. We read it in each other's eyes.

"Where are you guys?" she asked.

"In here, Mama," I said meekly.

She came to the bathroom and looked at Tony's ripped clothes and bloody scratches. She saw our red, tearful eyes. Her good mood turned sour in an instant.

"Oh, my God. What happened? What's going on?" she demanded.

Tony couldn't help himself and ran into her arms and sobbed. His little body shook as he told his scary tale.

"The old Sailor tried to grab me, Mama. I was stuck in the bushes and vines. I couldn't get away. I tried."

Mama held him and consoled him, but I could see the anger in her eyes. She looked at us both.

"I've had enough of this. No one will harm and scare my children. I'm going to go see that old coot, and I'm going to put a stop to this now," she said, with a fire that I wasn't used to seeing in her. "Let him try to scare me! Let him just try," she said.

"No, Mama, don't!" Tony pleaded.

"Mama, he has a mean dog. Don't go," I said.

But she went to the back porch and grabbed a garden hoe. "I'm not scared of his dog, or him."

Tony and I followed her out. She got into the car and placed the garden hoe beside her. We both jumped in the back seat.

"We're going with you," we told her.

She drove down the sandy path as far as it would let her. The Sailor's house was off the road, in the woods. She got out, taking the hoe with her.

"Stay here," she said.

Tony and I sat in the back seat, peering out the windshield, watching as she made her way into the trees.

"I should go with her," I said.

"Don't leave me, Amelia. I'm scared."

"It's okay, Tony," I said, though I felt scared, too.

Mama walked with defiance, not stopping until she reached the Sailor's porch. She knocked loudly on the old, gray door.

"Hello?" she called. "Come to the door." She stood and listened. Then she knocked again. "I know you're in there. I hear you!" She yelled. "So, you can scare little children, but you can't talk to a woman? Is that how you are?" Mama put her face closer to the door. "Listen, you, I'm telling you right now, *leave my kids alone!*"

There was a low growl. Mama clutched the garden hoe, ready to defend herself. She looked around as the growling became louder.

"You coward!" she yelled to the door. "Stay away from my kids!"

With that she backed off the porch, eyes still searching around for the dog. She turned and began to walk back down the path.

The old front door finally squeaked open. Mama turned back around. She stared, ready to encounter the old Sailor. But when she took one step back towards the porch and the door, it slammed shut so hard that Mama jumped.

The dog started barking.

"I've got to go help Mama," I told my terrified brother.

"Okay," he agreed. "Go."

I opened my door and ran down the path, the dog's barking growing louder. Mama was coming through the woods, looking behind her, ready to fight it off.

"Get to the car," she said.

7

Mama was still angry when we got back home. She grabbed the hoe out of the car and slammed the door.

"I'm calling the sheriff's office," she said, and stormed into the house. She went to the kitchen to use the phone.

Tony and I looked at each other. He was still wearing his torn and dirty clothes. I was in my big, damp t-shirt, my hair wild from the ride on the four-wheeler.

"We're a mess," I told him.

He looked down at himself. "My Batman shirt is toast," he said.

We tried to smile.

"I'm sorry I wasn't around to help you. I should've been," I said to him.

"It's okay, I didn't want you around, anyway." He grinned.

"Kids, the deputy is on his way." Mama was too wound up and nervous to sit down, so she crossed her arms and paced the floor until the deputy showed up.

After about fifteen minutes of Mama walking the floor, the deputy pulled into our drive.

Deputy Don Metcalf walked into our living room. He was big and tall, and had an easy presence.

"Good evening, folks," he said with a smile, and shook all our hands.

He and Mama sat at our kitchen table. She related everything that happened that day, and the strange noises we had heard during the storm. He listened patiently, writing notes.

"Tony, come here, please," Mama said. "Look at him. He was scared to death."

"Hi, son," Deputy Metcalf said to Tony. "You had a fright today, I see."

"Yes, sir, he tried to grab me, the old Sailor. He told me to get off his land. A dark haired lady parted the bushes for me and told me to run."

The deputy looked at his watch. "Well, I better take a trip over there before it gets dark. I'll find out what's going on. You all need to just try to relax. I'll be back shortly."

Deputy Metcalf pulled his cruiser to the same spot where Mama had parked. He got out and reached for his baton and secured it on his hip before closing the car door. He began his walk to the old house. Deep in the canopy of the live oak trees, the late-afternoon sun was already fading.

He made his way down the sandy path, listening, looking. He approached the house with caution. He looked to the front porch and decided to walk toward the rear, circling the entire house. He listened for noises, looked for any signs of life.

He walked onto the rickety back porch and peered through the glass window of the door. Through tattered curtains, he saw a dusty, unkempt kitchen. Rusty cans and old, yellowed newspapers littered the floor. He reached for the doorknob and it was locked tight. He then noticed a latch below the the doorknob and found the door was also locked and bolted from the outside.

He made his way around the house, peeking through every webbed and spidery window. He saw old, dusty furniture, and a few piles of clothes strewn about the floor. The windows were all locked and bolted down. He made his way to the front porch. He knocked loudly.

"Anybody in there?" He strained his ears to hear any movement.

"Hello!" He knocked again. There was total silence, except for the rustling of the trees in the breeze.

Just like the back door, the front door was locked and bolted from the outside. *It would be almost impossible to break into the house,* he thought.

The deputy stepped off the porch and started toward the rear of the house again. A small, broken-down barn sat in the backyard. The sun was going down, and it made eerie shadows fall over the property.

This place is creepy, he thought to himself.

He started for the barn and for a split second thought he saw a lady standing beside a shadowed tree.

"Hey! Hey, you!" he called out.

He ran to the tree and looked around. No one was there. No sound of anyone running through the woods. Silence. A chill ran down his back.

I'm just spooking myself, that's all. Get a grip, Don, he told himself.

He walked back to the barn and pushed open the rotted, wooden door. It opened with a loud squeak. He used his flashlight and scanned the interior. The only thing in there was a rusted tractor and more rusted tools. There were no signs of anyone staying in there, no poor vagrant looking for a place to sleep, no old Sailor.

He closed the door and searched around the back of the old barn. That's when he came upon a small, mounded grave. A sign had been placed as a headstone. The writing was etched and burned. It read: *Here lies Ol' Bruiser, a damn good dog.*

The deputy kind of grinned and shook his head at that. He was turning to leave when he heard a loud slam. It came from the back porch of the old house and stopped him in his tracks.

It couldn't be the door, he thought. *The door is bolted, it couldn't be.*

He ran to the back porch. The door was still locked and bolted, with no one in sight. He was ready to get out of there.

He made his way back to his patrol car, and frankly, was glad to be in it. He couldn't shake the strange feeling of being watched and followed the whole way down the path.

"Mrs. Williams, there is no one there," he told Mama, back at our house. "I did a thorough search of the entire property. No one."

"What about the mean dog?" I asked.

"I didn't see a dog, either." He thought about the dog's grave, Ol' Bruiser, but didn't mention that.

"I know someone was there. They slammed the door. It's not my imagination," Mama said.

Deputy Metcalf looked at Mama, concerned.

"Mrs. Williams, I'm not doubting you at all. Look, I'm going to have a deputy make extra patrols down this road. That property belongs to the Johnsons over in Beaufort, and I'm going to talk to them and see if they know what's going on. Until then, kids, stay out of the woods and off that property, okay?"

"Yes sir," we both said.

"And Mrs. Williams, if you see or hear anything at all, you call us and we will be here."

"I certainly will," Mama told him.

"I'll let you know what I find out as soon as possible," the deputy said. "Have a good evening, folks."

Deputy Metcalf pulled out of our drive. It was getting dark and he was happy to be leaving. He thought about everything as he drove: the figure by the trees, the slamming door.

You just got spooked, he told himself.

But he knew what he saw and heard and still couldn't shake that eerie feeling of being watched. His headlights caught a shape on the side of the road, then. He looked and saw a big dog watching him as he drove by.

8

I was four years older than Tony. We'd grown up taking care of each other. We were taught by our mother that nothing and no one was more important than family.

It was sometimes hard being a thirteen-year-old girl, and my Mama's biggest helper. But Mama always told us that we have to stick together, that as long as we had each other we would be fine.

She was right. We were okay. Some times were easier than others. Sometimes food was sparse and our clothes were worn, and our shoes a little snug. But we were together. Tony and I didn't complain. Mama did her best. That's what family was.

* * *

"I'm so bored," Tony whined.

"Me, too. Maybe Mama can take us to the library tomorrow to get some books."

"Yeah," Tony replied. "How long we gonna be holed up in this house?"

"I guess until Deputy Metcalf finds the old Sailor," I said.

"Will he put him in jail?" Tony asked.

"I hope so," I said.

Tony sat with his head in his hands. "I'm hot," he mumbled.

It was warm in this house. The sun beat down, the grass looked baked outside, and not one tiny whiff of a breeze stirred. I was hot, too. A box fan sat in front of the screen door, blowing in dry, hot air.

"Tony, go unplug the fan and bring it to me."

Tony dragged himself up and obeyed. "Where do you want it?"

I opened the refrigerator door and slid a kitchen chair in front of it. "Go grab two pillows off the couch," I told him.

He ran and got them.

"What are you doing?" he asked.

"You'll see."

I put the box fan on the chair in front of the opened door of the refrigerator, plugged it in, and turned it on. I put the pillows on the floor and I lay in front of the fan. Tony settled down beside me.

"Ahh, this feels like an air conditioner," Tony smiled.

We lay there on the cool tile and let the fan blow the cold air onto us. It was wonderful.

"Heaven," Tony said, with closed eyes.

"Tony, don't tell Mama."

"I won't."

* * *

Mama got the call from Deputy Metcalf at work.

"Mrs. Williams, I went and spoke to the Johnsons over in Beaufort today." He paused for just a moment. Mama held the phone close, waiting. "Joseph Johnson, the man you call the Sailor, died last winter. The family bolted down the house, and it's sat empty since then."

"But someone was there. I heard them walk. I heard the door slam. I know I did," Mama said.

"You know, Mrs. Williams, I thought I heard something, too. But no one was there. I did a thorough search. The doors are locked from the outside. Maybe it's time to call the Ghostbusters." He chuckled.

"What about a vagrant?" Mama wasn't in any mood for jokes. "What if vagrants are there?"

"I surely don't know how they'd get in that house. It's locked tighter than a tick. I promise, Mrs. Williams, there will be extra patrols in your area," he reassured her.

"Get a key," she insisted. "Get a key from the Johnson's or ask them to unlock it for you. Somebody is finding a way to get in there. Can you do that?" she asked.

"Yes, ma'am, I'll see what I can do."

Mama hung up the phone. "Ghostbusters," she said and shook her head. "Very funny."

The Sailor's Tale

9

Mama didn't have much to say when she got home from work. She had a tired and distant look in her eyes. She made us a small supper, but didn't eat. She sat on the front porch looking out across the field.

"Hard day, Mama?" I asked, walking out the screen door.

She held her arms out, wanting a hug. I hugged her tight.

"No, not too bad," she said with a slight smile. "I just worry, leaving you and your brother here alone. I wish I didn't have to."

She looked up and saw me staring out across the field.

"Mama...."

I pointed to the edge of the forest. A small and lonesome woman stood looking at us.

Mama looked. We both strained our eyes, frozen. Mama jumped up and started running to her. I couldn't move. My finger stayed pointed in the air.

She was not real. She stood like a statue, and then she was gone. She didn't run, she didn't move. I know she didn't, because my eyes were fixed on her. She just disappeared.

Mama was making her way across the field. She stopped and looked around. I took off after Mama.

"She must have run into the woods," Mama said, catching her breath. "See, there are vagrants in there. See."

I walked to the spot where the woman was standing. There sat the old, rusty sickle Tony had taken to the woods to build his fort. Beside the sickle was a little pile of freshly picked blackberries. I picked up the berries.

A gift? I wondered.

"What is this? Papa's old sickle? Blackberries?" Mama looked confused.

"Tony took the sickle with him when he went to build his fort. He left it in the woods."

I stared at the blackberries I held in my hand.

"The dark lady, she must have brought it back."

Mama picked up the sickle and stared into the woods. "Come on," she said. "Let's go home."

She walked, looking back often. When we reached the house, Tony was standing on the porch.

"What are you guys doing?" he asked.

"We found your Papa's sickle," Mama said, and went into the house and got on the phone.

The blackberries I held made bright red stains on my hands. I stared at them and started to tremble.

10

"Good morning, children." I opened the door to find Mr. Claude leaning on his cane and smiling. "Are you ready to go?" he asked.

Tony and I filed out of the house and got into his truck.

"Me and Mary Ann are so happy that you will be staying with us. We haven't had children in our house in a long time."

"Thank you for letting us stay with you while Mama works, it's very kind of you." I nudged Tony.

"Yes, thank you," he added.

"I hope you kids are hungry. Mary Ann has been so excited about you two coming over. She's preparing a big pancake breakfast."

"Yummy," I said, trying to sound excited.

We pulled down their drive and I noticed what a pretty little house they had. Trimmed bushes surrounded the house, and lots of tall trees shaded the yard. Many perfectly cared for flower beds adorned their property. A rather large vegetable garden sat in the backyard. A white picket fence with flowering vines of morning glory crawling up it surrounded the neat garden. It looked like a picture straight out of a storybook.

"Welcome, children," Mary Ann greeted us on the steps. "Please, come in."

She was all smiles. She did seem excited that we were here, and that felt good. I smiled back to her.

"You have a beautiful home," I told her.

Her house was bright and airy. The kitchen had clean, fresh, white cabinets, and red and white checked curtains hung in the windows. The little dining table was white with bright red cushioned chairs. The tile was a shiny, black and white checkerboard. Plants and flowers adorned every nook and cranny. It was a happy-looking place.

Mary Ann looked younger than Mr. Claude. She wore cotton pants and a cool, cotton blouse, tennis shoes and little ankle socks. Her hair was gray and cut short and simple. Her eyes smiled.

She led us into a foyer and showed us a table where we could put our things.

"Let's eat before it gets cold, and then I will show you around. I want you both to feel at home here," she said.

I looked and Tony had a smile from ear to ear. I could tell he felt good being here, too.

The breakfast was incredible: pancakes and bacon, juice, and fruit. Her bowls and plates were all different bright colors, yellow, orange, red, and green.

Mr. Claude rose when he saw she needed coffee. He refilled it for her and gave her a little kiss on the top of her head. She smiled at him and placed her hand on top of his, just for a moment. It was sweet.

So this is what love looks like, I thought to myself.

"So, how about we go to the beach today?" Mr. Claude asked. "We could act like tourists." He chuckled.

"Let's ask the children. What would you like to do?" Mary Ann asked.

We honestly thought we would be sitting here all summer, watching the two old people nap and watch the news. Tony and I had resigned ourselves that we would be miserable here.

"The beach sounds fun," Tony said.

"Yes, it does," I added.

* * *

Mama picked us up at five. She came to the door and heard us all laughing at Mr. Claude playing a silly song on the piano. We had red noses from our day on the beach and smiles on our faces.

"Come in, Angela," Mary Ann offered.

"No, that's okay. You guys have had a full day, I'm sure. We'll get out of your hair," Mama said.

"We've had a wonderful day, and I'm sure you must be tired and ready to go home. I'll get the children for you," Mary Ann told her.

11

It rained hard for three days. We stayed inside and found things to do.

Mary Ann had several bookshelves that we explored, finding lots to read. Mr. Claude taught us how to play the card game Rummy, and Tony was hooked. After several rounds, we all told Tony we needed a break. Mary Ann fixed oyster stew and cornbread muffins for lunch.

We sat around the little table, eating while the rain poured down.

"I haven't wanted to bring this up to you two, since I know you have been very scared with everything that's been going on at your house. But I think we need to talk about it," Mr. Claude said seriously. "I know you thought the old Sailor tried to grab you, Tony, but that cannot be. Joseph Johnson, the one you call the old Sailor, doesn't live there anymore."

"He doesn't?" Tony asked.

Mr. Claude paused and thought about the next thing he needed to say. "Tony, Joseph Johnson died last December. His family took him to Beaufort and buried him there."

"What about the lady, the lady with the dark hair?" Tony asked.

"She's a ghost," I blurted out. "I saw her. She stood on the edge of the woods. She stood like a statue and she disappeared. She didn't run away. She disappeared. I saw it."

Everyone turned to me. I had tears in my eyes. It was the first time I told anyone about that day, even though it haunted me.

Mary Ann rose from her chair and came to me. She hugged my neck and patted my head.

"I believe you," she said. "There are lost spirits, I know. You need to know, children, that I knew Joseph Johnson. He wasn't a bad man. He was a good man. He worked on a ship that sailed all over the world, delivering and buying goods. He met his wife, Maria, in Spain. He brought her back here to live, but his job took him away a lot. She became sad and wanted to go home. All the trinkets and clothes and jewelry he brought back to her from his travels didn't please her. She missed her family and her home."

"Why didn't he let her go home?" I asked, wiping my eyes.

"He was madly in love with her, and I think it drove him a little mad. He couldn't let her go. He should have," Mr. Claude said. "Many years ago, Joseph was out to sea when Maria became sick with influenza. His sister attended to her and nursed her, but she didn't live. His family said she didn't want to live, and willed herself to die. When he came home they had already buried her, right on the property across from your house. Joseph was a broken man. It was then that he became sort of a hermit. He let himself go and grew a long beard. He was dirty and his clothes were torn and tattered. He let his beautiful house and property fall into decay. He was an old friend, but when I'd see him, he wouldn't talk. He was, in a way, already dead."

"I have seen Maria, too, Amelia," Mary Ann said. "I was walking through the woods, just enjoying a sunny day, taking a hike, when I heard a soft cry. It sounded like a young woman or girl. I walked through the bushes and vines. I searched until I came upon a dark-haired girl, kneeling, hands over her eyes, sobbing. She looked straight at me and said, 'I want to go home.' After that, she disappeared. I was more sad than scared, I think, because I couldn't help her."

"Joseph is back now because Maria is still there. He will not leave her," Mr. Claude added.

"We need to help Maria get home. Somehow, we need to help her," I said.

"Okay, you guys are freaking me out!" Tony said. "Ghosts? Really? I'm shaking, here. My body is totally trembling."

I put my arm around Tony.

"Maria came here from the sea," Mary Ann said. "Maybe the sea will release her."

"What do you mean?" I asked.

"We need to get in the house and find something that belonged to her and release it to the sea. The sea will take her home."

12

Mama didn't have to be at work until four at the seafood restaurant. Tony and I paced nervously, waiting to go to Mr. Claude and Mary Ann's house.

Our plan was made. Mr. Claude would go to the house and get in. He would look for something that had belonged to Maria. He would then pick us up and the four of us would drive to Fort Macon beach and throw it in the ocean. We hoped this would release Maria and allow her to finally go home and rest, and allow the old Sailor to rest, too.

"Are you kids ready?" Mama asked.

"Yes," we said, and ran to the car.

* * *

Mr. Claude was getting ready to leave when we got to his house.

"Let's get this over with," he said. He grabbed his cane and started to the truck.

"I want to go with you," I said.

He looked at me. "Are you sure?" he asked.

"Yes, I want to help her, help Maria," I said. "Tony, stay here with Mary Ann, I'll be okay."

"We're supposed to stay together, Amelia," he said.

"I'll be back soon, I promise. I'll be fine."

I jumped in the truck and put my feet up on a big toolbox.

"What's this for?" I asked.

"I don't know if the house is locked up. I might need a tool," Mr. Claude replied.

We stopped on the path and started through the woods. I lugged the heavy toolbox. We arrived to the old house and Mr. Claude didn't hesitate as he walked to the door. He inspected the knob.

"Locked up like Fort Knox," he said. "Bring me the toolbox, Amelia."

He rifled through the tools and finally picked one out. "This might work," he said.

Just then, the growling started.

"The mean dog," I whispered.

"Go away, Bruiser, you're dead," Mr. Claude yelled.

The growl was low and mean.

"I should've shot you ten years ago when you killed my best hen, now go away!" he yelled even louder.

The growling stopped.

He found a bolt cutter and strained to cut the lock. I stood beside him, wishing I could help. Something banged in the house. I looked at Mr. Claude, but he didn't stop trying to break that lock.

"Is that you, Claude Pelletier?" It was Deputy Don.

I turned around, surprised.

"Yes, it is," Mr. Claude answered.

"What are you doing?" the deputy asked.

"I'm trying to open this dang door," he said.

Deputy Don started up the porch."You do realize this is breaking and entering, do you not?"

"I reckon it is," Mr. Claude said. "I don't know if you realize this, but we've got a ghost problem, and I'm trying to fix it."

"Claude," Deputy Don started, but stopped when the door started shaking.

It shook so hard it looked like it was going to explode. We all took a step back and held our eyes wide. Another loud bang was heard inside the house, like something heavy fell to the floor.

The deputy knocked loudly on the door. "Who's in there?" he yelled.

Silence.

He reached in his pants pocket and pulled out a key. He grabbed the lock, and I noticed his hands were shaking slightly. He unlocked it and opened the door. A cold like I've never felt flew into our faces. The deputy peered in. Mr. Claude shuffled by him and walked in.

"Joseph Johnson," he said. "It's your friend, Claude Pelletier." An old clock that sat on a mantel flew through the air, barely missing him. "I just want to help you. You need to rest. Maria needs to rest."

Every door in that dark place started banging, blasting the noise through the house.

Help me, I heard a small voice whisper from the hallway. *Help me...*

I ran toward the door. I tried to open it. It wasn't locked, but it felt like someone was standing on the other side holding it shut. I pushed as hard as I could.

Deputy Don grabbed me. "Move," he said.

He took his large body and shoved it open.

GO AWAY! An angry voice growled, low and evil.

The whole house began to shake. Mr. Claude was having trouble standing with his cane.

I looked around the room. I could tell it was once beautiful. It now sat dusty and rotting. I looked at an old dressing table. A locket sat open. I picked it up. Two pictures, one of a beautiful, dark-haired woman, the other of a handsome man.

Maria's mother and father, I thought. No, I knew.

I grabbed the locket and started to run out the door. What felt like two strong hands landed on my my shoulders and shoved me hard. I flew backward and fell to the floor.

Deputy Don ran to me. "Let's get out of here," he yelled over the noise of the shaking house and the banging doors.

I looked and the locket sat on the floor beside me. I went to grab it and it flew across the room. I started crawling toward it.

"The locket!" I screamed. I grabbed it just in time, as Deputy Don picked me up and started running to the front door.

"Out, now!" he yelled to Mr. Claude.

Mr. Claude started making his way to the door with the help of his cane.

"I got something!" I told him. "Let's go!"

It was then that the front door slammed shut. The deputy pushed and pushed to open it.

"Back up," he said, and kicked it as hard as he could. The whole door flew off its hinges. We ran.

We made our way up the path. None of us spoke. What could we say? I clutched the locket tight in my hand.

Ahead of us stood a dark figure, blocking the path. We stopped.

"Let us pass, Joseph," Mr. Claude yelled. "If you love Maria, let her rest. Let her go home. Give her that, Joseph."

The dark figure started to fade. It grew smaller and smaller, until all that was left was a small light. The small light flickered like a match and slowly went out.

We made it to the end of the path and met Tony and Mary Ann, who were coming to check on us.

I hugged my brother. I showed Mary Ann the locket.

"You did well," she said. "Let's go."

13

"Get in my car. I'll take you where you need to go."

"Fort Macon beach," I told the deputy.

We made it to Fort Macon. We all got out. I couldn't run like I wanted to. Instead, I waited for Mr. Claude to make his way down.

I went to a rocky point and grabbed Tony's hand. "Come with me," I said.

We got as far as we could. The ocean's spray hit our faces. I reared my arm back and flung the locket with all my might.

"Go home, Maria," I said. "Be at peace."

A beautiful light appeared above the waves, darting and dancing. We all watched in awe. The light played on the water, glowing brightly, before it suddenly shot skyward.

Home... a soft voice whispered.

* * *

Mama finally had a day off, on a beautiful Saturday. She was busy washing clothes and scrubbing the bathroom. She wore an old pair of blue jean shorts and a t-shirt. Her hair was tied up in a red bandanna. Tony ran for the back door.

"Hold on a minute, Tony, where are you going in such an all-out hurry?" Mama asked.

"I'm going fishing with Mr. Claude. We gotta catch his supper, he told me," Tony answered.

"Oh, okay, don't be late, and be careful," she said.

"I won't and I will," he answered, and flew out the door.

Mama grabbed the mop bucket and began to fill it up. I started out the door.

"See you in a little while," I said. "And yes, my room is cleaned."

She turned from the bucket. "What are your plans?" she asked.

"Me and Mary Ann are going to pick blackberries. She's going to teach me how to make jelly."

"Okay, I'll see you later," she said, turning back to fill the bucket.

I made it halfway down our drive. I stopped. I went back to the house.

"Mama?"

"Yes?" Mama answered.

"Do you want to go with us?" I asked.

Mama turned from the sink and looked at me. She pulled the bandanna from her hair.

"Yes," she said. "Yes, I do."

We walked, arm in arm, the whole way to Mary Ann's lovely house.

About The Author

Jennie Ford is a mother, writer, potter, and artist. Jennie was raised in Eastern North Carolina, where the rich farming landscapes provide the backdrop to many of her stories.

As a contributor to Storyshares for many years, she will continue to compose short stories for their expanding library. Now residing in Western North Carolina, Jennie is currently writing a novel for young adult readers, which she hopes to publish in the future.

About The Publisher

Story Shares is a nonprofit focused on supporting the millions of teens and adults who struggle with reading by creating a new shelf in the library specifically for them. The ever-growing collection features content that is compelling and culturally relevant for teens and adults, yet still readable at a range of lower reading levels.

Story Shares generates content by engaging deeply with writers, bringing together a community to create this new kind of book. With more intriguing and approachable stories to choose from, the teens and adults who have fallen behind are improving their skills and beginning to discover the joy of reading. For more information, visit storyshares.org.

Easy to Read. Hard to Put Down.

www.ingramcontent.com/pod-product-compliance
Lightning Source LLC
Chambersburg PA
CBHW051313170626
46809CB00004B/1872